Anatomy of a

FLOOD

by Terri Dougherty

Content Consultant:
Donna Charlevoix, PhD
Director, Science & Education Division
The GLOBE Program
University Corporation for Atmospheric Research
Boulder, Colorado

CAPSTONE PRESS
a capstone imprint

Velocity is published by Capstone Press,
151 Good Counsel Drive, P.O. Box 669, Mankato, Minnesota 56002.
www.capstonepub.com

 Books published by Capstone Press are manufactured with paper
containing at least 10 percent post-consumer waste.

Library of Congress Cataloging-in-Publication Data
Dougherty, Terri.
  Anatomy of a flood/by Terri Dougherty.
  p. cm.—(Velocity. disasters)
  Includes bibliographical references and index.
  Summary: "Describes floods, including their causes, prediction, and effects"—provided
by publisher.
  ISBN 978-1-4296-6021-1 (library binding)
  ISBN 978-1-4296-7355-6 (paperback)
  1.Floods—Juvenile literature. I. Title

GB1399.D68 2012
551.48'9—dc22   2010049204

Editorial Credits: Pam Mamsch
Art Director: Suzan Kadribasic
Designers: Deepika Verma, Manish Kumar

Photo Credits
Alamy: Freefall Images, 14 (middle right), Ryan McGinnis, 30 (top), Pat Canova, 32, Jeff
Greenberg, 44; AP Photo: Brian Chilson, 5, Sue Ogrocki, 6-7, Tom Stromme/The Bismarck
Tribune, 20 (top), Sue Ogrocki, 20 (bottom); Corbis: Bettmann, 16-17, U.S. Coast Guard/
Science Faction, 21; Dreamstime: Cook, 8–9; ESO: G. Gillet, 31 (bottom); European
Space Agency: 31 (top); FEMA: Susie Shapira, 14 (top), Jacinta Quesada, 14 (middle
left), Robert Kaufmann, 14 (bottom), Patsy Lynch, 15, David Fine, 18 (bottom), Marvin
Nauman, 19, Jocelyn Augustino, 24-25; Istockphoto: Jerry Schiller, 28-29, Mike Clarke,
30 (bottom); Library of Congress: 35; NASA: Jesse Allen/Earth Observatory 38 (bottom),
39 (top); National Archives and Records Administration: 40; NOAA Photo Library:
Providence Journal Co., cover (front), 23; Shutterstock: Rex Rover, cover (background),
Mary Terriberry, 11, KennStilger47, 18 (top), Brendan Reals, 27, Paul Orr, 43 (flashlight),
Creative Images, 43 (can), Ifong, 43 (bottle), Restyler, 43 (batteries), Tobias Machhaus, 43
(radio), Lusoimages, 43 (top); U.S. Army: 45; Wikipedia: USGS/Austin Post, 26, DVIC/
SSgt Paul Griffin, 38–39.

Printed in the United States of America in Melrose Park, Illinois.
032011   006112LKF11

TABLE OF CONTENTS

WALL OF WATER

Screams told Nick Hofert something was wrong. Terrified families were rushing toward his hillside cabin. They were desperately trying to escape the rising water flooding the valley below.

Heavy rain had swelled the Caddo and Little Missouri rivers. On the night of June 11, 2010, a wall of water rushed toward an Arkansas campground. Many campers were asleep as the water rose as much as 8 feet (2.4 m) in one hour. The water was waist deep when Hertha Whatley and her family left their camper. She was almost sucked under a floating car as she tried to climb to higher ground. Whatley and 19 family members linked arms as they waded through water to the top of a hill.

Another couple survived by parking their pickup truck between two trees. They rode out the flood in the back of the truck as it bobbed up and down in the water. Others were not as fortunate. Twenty people were killed by the waters that rushed over the campground.

Floods can strike with deadly force. Rushing water can uproot trees, carry away cars, and wipe out bridges. Floods are a destructive, and often surprising, force of nature. Water can rise quickly, giving people little time to escape. Floods kill more people than any other weather-related disaster. Surging floodwaters can swiftly bring devastation.

A flash flood can destroy anything in its path, including campers and other vehicles.

Chapter 1

NATURAL HAZARD

What is a Flood?

Hours of steady rain soaked Oklahoma City, Oklahoma, in June 2010. Water flowed down roads, over bridges, and into yards. There was so much water that people floated down the street in boats. Water seeped into homes and businesses. The area was flooded.

A flood occurs when water covers land that is usually dry. The ground cannot absorb the water. Not every flood is the same. A flood may be a few inches or many feet deep. The water may arrive suddenly or creep slowly higher. Sometimes the water drains away quickly. Other times an area stays flooded for weeks.

FACT: It takes only 6 inches (15 cm) of fast-moving water to knock someone off his or her feet. A car or truck can be swept away by 2 feet (61 cm) of water.

Floods have many causes. They can occur when:
- Melting snow causes a river to rise steadily. The water overflows its banks, creeping into nearby fields and homes. The flooding may linger for days or weeks.
- Heavy rainfall makes a river rise quickly, sending a surge of water pouring down a hillside.
- A dam breaks and releases the water it had been holding.
- A **hurricane** or strong storm pushes water onto the coast.
- A large amount of rain falls onto dry, hard soil.
- Heavy rainfall brings more water than a city's sewer system can carry away. The flood fills city streets and water may flow into people's driveways, yards, and homes.

FLOOD DANGER

People are often not aware of the power of a flood. Floods are dangerous and may come with little warning. Rapidly flowing water can carry away cars and trucks. A person may be swept away by rushing water. About 127 people are killed by floods each year in the United States.

hurricane—a spinning storm with winds of 74 miles (119 km) per hour or more

Where Do Floods Happen?

Floods can occur almost anywhere. Low land near a river is more likely to be flooded than higher ground far from a body of water.

Even a small body of water, however, can swell and flood the surrounding areas. If there is hard, rocky soil on the side of a mountain, the water from a heavy rain cannot soak into the ground. It flows downward, into the valley. A mountain stream that is usually only a few inches deep can quickly rise and become a raging river.

An area that has more rain than usual over weeks or months is also in danger of flooding. Up to 30 inches (76 cm) of rain fell on Iowa in May and June 2008. The rain brought floods to many areas and covered almost 10 square miles (26 square km) of Cedar Rapids.

Rain does not need to fall directly on an area for it to be in danger of flooding. A powerful storm high in the mountains can bring rain that makes a river rise. The high water rushes toward the valley below, where people may not be aware of the dangerous high water that is approaching.

A flood can even occur in areas where the soil is normally very dry. The ground in these areas is hard. When rain comes, the water cannot soak into the hard ground. A rainstorm in the desert can quickly cause dry creek beds to fill with water.

Hard, rocky soil on the sides of mountains can't absorb heavy rainfall. The water runs down and floods the valley below.

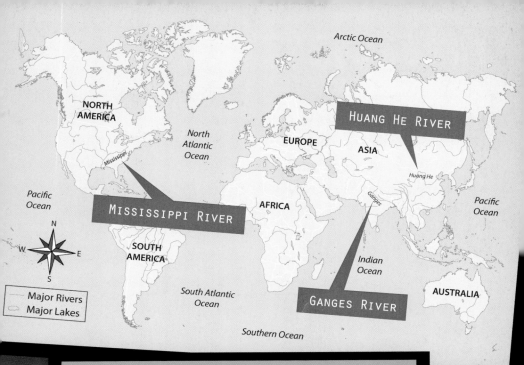

When water from a large area drains into a river, the land near that river is more likely to be flooded. Some rivers that take in water from large areas are the Mississippi River in the United States, the Ganges River in India, and the Huang He River in China.

The Huang He River sometimes becomes clogged with silt. The river changes course to get around the blocked area and floods the land.

Experts can create maps of an area that show which areas will be in danger as a river rises. They look at the height of the land throughout the area. They also look at how water is expected to flow. They use computer software to analyze this data. The software is used to create maps to show which areas and neighborhoods could be flooded.

Floodplains

The land next to a river that is most likely to flood is called the floodplain. The land in a floodplain is usually dry. When the river rises, the water goes into the floodplain. In rare cases, water from a flood can spread beyond the floodplain.

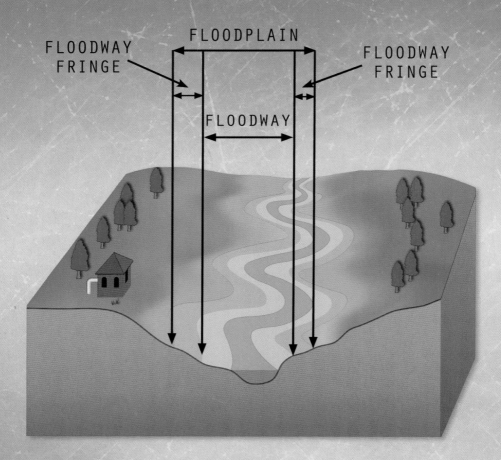

The floodplain is important. It provides a place for water to go when snow melts or heavy rain falls. This water helps carry nutrients to the floodplain's soil. The nutrients make it easier for plants to grow.

The area closest to the river is called the floodway. The water here will probably be moving when a flood occurs. The area at the edge of the floodplain is called the floodway fringe. The fringe area will probably have standing water during a flood. People must be careful when building homes and buildings near a river. They should not build in the floodplain. When a river goes over its banks, everything in the floodplain will be affected.

CAN FLOODS HELP?

Floods have a helpful side. The water carries bits of material that settles on the land. This sediment enriches the soil and makes it fertile to help plants grow.

Floods can also help control **erosion**. When floodwaters spread over a large area, the water flows more slowly than it would if it was in a narrow riverbed. Less soil is worn away from riverbanks when water moves slowly.

Flooded areas are also important resting spots for animals. Birds flying north or south stop in flooded fields and wetlands to eat. An oil spill covered nesting areas along the U.S. Gulf Coast in 2010. Farmers were asked to flood fields so birds would have places to rest and find food.

erosion—the process of wearing away rock or soil by water, wind, or ice

11

In Season, Any Season

Floods can happen at any time of the year, but they are more common at certain times. Flood season is the time of the year when rivers are most likely to flow over their banks.

Areas that get heavy rain at certain times of the year risk getting flooded. California gets most of its rain between late October and March. Moisture from the Pacific Ocean moves inland at this time of the year. When it reaches California's mountains, the warm, moist air is forced to rise. It cools as it rises, creating clouds and rainstorms.

Flash floods may occur after a summer thunderstorm brings a large amount of rain. In the southwest United States, southerly winds blow more moisture into the area during July and August. This increases the risk of monsoons and flash floods.

monsoon—a wind that blows at certain times of the year; during monsoon season, there is very heavy rainfall

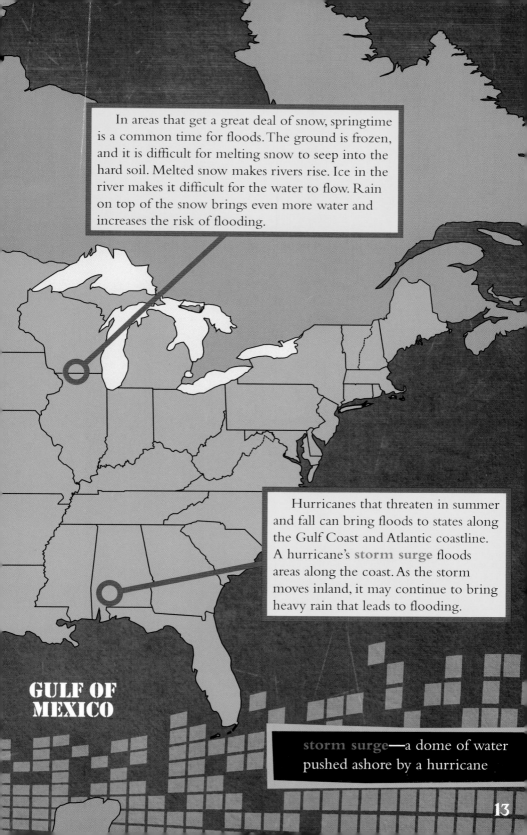

In areas that get a great deal of snow, springtime is a common time for floods. The ground is frozen, and it is difficult for melting snow to seep into the hard soil. Melted snow makes rivers rise. Ice in the river makes it difficult for the water to flow. Rain on top of the snow brings even more water and increases the risk of flooding.

Hurricanes that threaten in summer and fall can bring floods to states along the Gulf Coast and Atlantic coastline. A hurricane's **storm surge** floods areas along the coast. As the storm moves inland, it may continue to bring heavy rain that leads to flooding.

GULF OF
MEXICO

storm surge—a dome of water
pushed ashore by a hurricane

Flood Costs

It doesn't take long for a flood to become costly. An entire building may be washed away by rapidly moving water. A road can crack, buckle, or be destroyed when water rushes over it. Water can sweep away or damage cars and trucks. Crops die when floodwaters cover farms.

A flood can wash a home off its foundation.

Floods can destroy farmers' crops.

Floods also cause problems when water seeps into homes and businesses. Furniture becomes soggy. Carpeting is soaked. A layer of mud covers everything.

Floods are expensive disasters. They cause billions of dollars in damage in the United States each year.

Floods cost the United States $5 billion in 2008. What could you buy with $5 billion?

2 Yankee stadiums
+ 10,000 sports cars
+ 20 million video games

Chapter 2

TYPES OF FLOODS

Flash Floods

On July 31, 1976, thousands of people were enjoying the beautiful scenery of the Big Thompson Canyon in Colorado. Heavy rain began to fall at about 6 p.m. The storm poured more than 7 inches (18 cm) of rain into the canyon in just an hour.

The canyon's rock walls could not absorb the water. The Big Thompson River swelled from its normal level of 2 feet (61 cm) to a wall of water 10 to 15 feet (3 to 4.6 m) high. It sped down the mountain, taking boulders, buildings, cars, and campers with it. Within two hours, the highway was washed out. More than 400 houses and 150 businesses were destroyed. The flood killed 145 people and caused more than $40 million in damage.

A flash flood like the one that surged through Big Thompson Canyon is rapid and deadly. It sends a torrent of water ripping through an area. Intense rainfall is often at the heart of a flash flood. It causes a river to quickly rise, and the water rushes downstream.

A flash flood can also occur when a dam bursts and suddenly releases a gush of water. It is difficult to warn people that the water is coming because the flood happens so suddenly.

MORE THAN WATER

As a flash flood rushes down a mountain, it picks up whatever is in its path. The wall of water could be carrying

- BOULDERS
- MUD
- TREES
- CARS
- HOMES

Water surges down Big Thompson Canyon.

Regional Floods

More than 13 inches (33 cm) of rain overwhelmed the Cumberland River in early May 2010. After two days of rain, the river rose 12 feet (3.7 m) above flood level. It spilled over its banks and soaked Nashville, Tennessee, and other cities in the area. The river stayed above flood level for days.

A regional flood like the one that hit Nashville affects a large area. It is often caused by a long period of wet weather or melting snow. The ground cannot absorb any more water, and the river overflows. Businesses close, and people must leave their homes. The high water lingers, making it impossible to travel down roads. It can be weeks or months before a regional flood subsides.

the 2010 Nashville flood

FACT

Regional floods destroy more property than flash floods. But flash floods are deadlier than regional floods. Flash floods are the top weather-related killer in the United States.

NASHVILLE FLOOD TIMELINE

MAY 1

Heavy rain begins to fall. Neighborhoods begin to flood and roads close. Five people drown.

RIVER LEVEL: 19 feet (5.8 m)

MAY 2

Roads become rivers as rain pours down. The Cumberland River is almost at its flood stage of 36 feet (11 m).

RIVER LEVEL: 35 feet (10.7 m)

MAY 3

The water reaches its peak level. Muddy water fills downtown Nashville. The death toll rises to 18.

RIVER LEVEL: Almost 52 feet (15.8 m)

MAY 4

Roads remain covered with water. A plant where water is cleaned has been damaged. People are asked to use as little water as possible.

RIVER LEVEL: 50 feet (15.2 m)

MAY 5

People begin to return to their homes, but some areas remain flooded. Concerts raise money to help people rebuild. Thousands of people volunteer to help clean up the mess.

RIVER LEVEL: 48 feet (14.6 m)

MAY 6

The flood has killed 21 people, including a 19-year-old man who tried to raft on the floodwaters.

RIVER LEVEL: 43 feet (13.1 m)

MAY 7

The Cumberland River has dropped below flood stage.

RIVER LEVEL: 35 feet (10.7 m)

MAY 8

Volunteers help residents clean up buildings damaged by the floods.

RIVER LEVEL: 29 feet (8.8 m)

Ice Jam Floods

A wall of ice blocked the Missouri River in March 2009. Chunks of ice as large as cars kept the water from moving downstream. It had nowhere to go except over its banks and into the city of Bismarck, North Dakota. To get the water moving again, crews used explosives to blast the ice jam apart.

Ice jam floods can occur when ice begins to freeze in winter or thaw in spring. Ice chunks moving down the river get caught in a shallow area or a bend in the river. They can pile up behind logs or bridge supports. The pile of ice creates a dam that blocks water and ice flowing toward it. The river overflows its banks when water and ice can no longer flow downstream.

A jam can cause more trouble when the water bursts through the ice dam. If water is released quickly, it rushes downstream, causing a flash flood. The mixture of water and ice chunks can cause serious damage to buildings and bridges. The cold water can be deadly to anyone in its way.

A firefighter rescues a flood victim.

Icebreaker boat

BREAKING UP THE ICE

There are several ways to break up an ice jam.

ICE CUTTING: When a river is covered with ice, slots are cut into it with special saws. This helps the ice break up and move downstream when it begins to melt.

BLASTING: Explosives are used to smash the ice jam and get water flowing.

ICE BREAKING: A vehicle such as an icebreaker boat or a crane with a wrecking ball is used to crush the ice cover so it can flow downstream.

Storm Surge Floods

A powerful hurricane battered Galveston Island, Texas, on the night of September 8, 1900. Winds of 140 miles (225 km) per hour whipped across the island. A deadly storm surge developed. A dome of water almost 16 feet (5 m) high swept over the island. It crushed buildings and carried people into the water. As many as 8,000 people died that night, and 3,600 buildings were destroyed.

As a hurricane rotates, its wind pushes water toward the shore. This dome of water can be taller than a house. On top are waves driven by the wind. The surge dome can be anywhere from 50 to 100 miles (80 to 161 km) wide. When it hits land, it is deadly and destructive. The storm surge is strong enough to wash away homes and piers. It can wash away roads, railroads, and beaches.

HOW A SURGE HAPPENS

1. The hurricane's winds turn around the center of the storm, called the eye.

2. The eye has the lowest pressure of the storm. There is less air pressing down on the water here. The water near the center of the hurricane rises. It forms a mound.

3. At the same time, the hurricane's strong wind is pushing the water as the hurricane turns.

4. The mound of water in the center of the hurricane and the water pushed by the wind form a bulge of water. It can flow away in deep water.

5. The ocean is shallower near the shore. The bulge of water cannot flow away.

6. A dome of water rises to the side of the storm.

7. The dome and waves on top of it pound the coast. The surge is higher if it arrives at the same time as high tide.

TSUNAMIS

Deadly **tsunamis** can strike with little warning. A tsunami in the Indian Ocean on December 26, 2004, killed 180,000 people. In March 2011, a large earthquake off the coast of Japan triggered a 23-foot (7-m) tsunami. The huge wave swept away cars, homes, and boats. The earthquake and tsunami killed more than 18,000 people.

A tsunami can be horribly destructive. The waves are set in motion by an earthquake or the eruption of a volcano. As the waves near land, they grow and become a wall of water. When the wave hits the shore, a powerful flood is created. The flood sweeps away everything in its path. The water drains back into the ocean, and soon another large wave hits the shore.

tsunami—a giant sea wave

Hurricane Camille brought a 24-foot (7-m) storm surge to Pass Christian, Mississippi, on August 17, 1969. The surge impacted the towns of Waveland and Bay St. Louis 8 miles (13 km) inland.

Dam and Levee Failure Floods

The city of New Orleans, Louisiana, is below sea level. **Levees** were built along the banks of lakes and canals to keep water away from the city. Levees are structures that hold back water. They are usually made of a pile of rock and soil that is covered with concrete. They are built high enough to keep water from flooding an area.

On August 29, 2005, Hurricane Katrina hit New Orleans with an intense storm surge. The surge was too much for some levees. They gave way, and water poured into the city. Homes, businesses, and roads were covered with water. Many people drowned when they could not escape the flood.

When levees hold, they help prevent floods. Temporary levees made of sandbags are sometimes built along rising rivers to keep water away. A levee that breaks, however, is dangerous. It can create a flash flood that puts lives and property in danger.

levee—a bank built up to prevent flooding

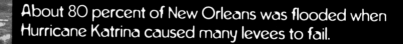
About 80 percent of New Orleans was flooded when Hurricane Katrina caused many levees to fail.

DAM AND LEVEE FAILURE

In a match with a dam or levee and water, sometimes the water wins. Here are some types of dam and levee failures:

1. Water flows over the top.

2. Water seeps through.

3. Wind and water wear the levee down.

4. Water erodes the soil under the dam or levee.

DAM FAILURE FLOODS

Dams hold back flowing water. They are often used to help convert the power of moving water into electricity. The water held back by dams creates lakes. These lakes can supply drinking water for cities and are also good places for boating, fishing, and swimming.

If a dam fails to hold the water back, however, a flood can result. If a dam collapses, it allows the water it was holding back to rush downstream.

Debris, Landslide, and Mudflow Floods

Mount St. Helens erupted on May 18, 1980. The volcano's blast and hot ash melted snow and ice. Within minutes, a flood of water, boulders, and mud was rushing down the mountain. As the surge flowed down, it toppled trees. It also crushed roads, homes, and bridges. The debris it carried clogged the Toutle River. Soon the river was 21 feet (6.4 m) above its normal level. In the Muddy River, the mudflow was more than 33 feet (10 m) deep.

The eruption of Mount St. Helens sent a flow of mud and debris down the side of the mountain.

debris—the remains of something that has been destroyed

The eruption of a volcano can trigger a flood filled with debris. The fast-moving water rips out trees, picks up rocks, and erodes soil and sand. The debris becomes trapped in the water. This mixture is called a lahar. As it moves, it looks like wet concrete.

A landslide or lahar can clog rivers with a mass of dirt, rocks, and logs. More flooding occurs behind the dam. When the dam bursts, a flash flood occurs as the released water rushes downstream.

the Kautz Glacier on Mount Rainier

GLACIAL FLOODS

A flood of debris can also occur when water trapped by a glacier is suddenly released. This is called an outburst flood. The rush of water creates landslides. Rocks, trees, brush, and dirt mix with the water. The ground shakes as the mixture roars down the mountain.

In 1947 heavy rain started an outburst flood on the Kautz Glacier on Mount Rainier in the state of Washington. The flood ripped away part of the glacier and carved a 300-foot (91-m) canyon in the ice.

lahar—a flow of water mixed with debris from a volcano
glacier—a large, slow moving mass of ice

Chapter 3

PREDICTING A FLOOD

Stormy Weather

Rain clouds and thunderstorms bring downpours that can create floods. What triggers strong storms?

Drops of moisture in the air **condense** when warm air rises. These droplets form clouds. Inside the cloud, the droplets combine into larger drops. They fall as raindrops when they become too heavy to be held up by an updraft of wind. Rain also falls when ice crystals inside the cloud fall and melt on the way down. Winds blowing in different directions or at different speeds help the storm grow. The winds let more warm, moist air rise into the storm.

Sometimes one storm after another will hit the same area in a short amount of time. This is known as "storm training." Training storms soak the ground with water and cause flooding.

condense—to turn from a gas to a liquid

Of course, not every storm brings a flood. Whether or not a flood occurs depends on a number of things, including the following:

- The amount of water already in the soil. If the soil is too wet, no more water can soak into it. If it is too dry, the water will run off rather than be absorbed by the soil.
- The rate at which the rain falls. If a lot of rain falls in a short amount of time, the area is more likely to flood.
- The type of surface the rain hits. Rain will soak into ground covered with grass, but it cannot soak into ground covered by pavement. The water will run off of pavement or concrete, and must be carried away in a ditch or underground sewer.

THE 100-YEAR FLOOD

A major flood is sometimes called a 100-year flood. It does not mean that a severe flood hits exactly every 100 years. The term means there is a 1 in 100 chance (1 percent) that an area will experience a flood of this intensity in any year.

FACT

One of the worst thunderstorms in U.S. history hit Fort Worth, Texas, in May 1995. The storm's flash floods and lightning killed 100 people. The storm caused damage worth $2 billion.

Forecasting Tools

Weather forecasters use tools to help predict storms and floods. **DOPPLER RADAR** uses an antenna that sends out microwave beams. Raindrops in a storm cloud reflect this beam. Computers use this information to figure out the direction and speed of a storm.

RAIN GAUGES collect water and let forecasters know how much rain has fallen in an area.

COMPUTER MODELS use information on wind direction, air moisture, temperature, and air pressure to create models. The models show which areas may have storms in the next few days.

radar—a system that uses radio waves to detect and locate objects

SATELLITE images show forecasters where clouds are present. Some satellites can also measure how much moisture is in the soil.

WATCHES AND WARNINGS

A flood watch is issued by the National Weather Service when the weather is right for a flood to occur in an area. The watch is broadcast on TV, radio, and the Internet. Flash floods can arrive quickly. People need to be ready to leave when the water starts to rise.

A flood warning means that an area is experiencing flooding or flooding will begin soon. People should move to a safe location immediately when a warning is issued.

PRECIPITATION OBSERVATIONS

of how much rain, snow, or hail has fallen in the past day show which areas are getting more rain than usual. These observations are made both by instruments and by people who keep track of the weather in their own backyards.

WEATHER BALLOONS

are sent into the air by the National Weather Service. They carry instruments that measure wind speed and direction, air pressure, humidity levels, and temperature.

satellite—a spacecraft that circles Earth and takes pictures of the planet from space

Tracking High Water

River gages are also important tools for predicting floods. Gages measure the depth of rivers. They also measure how fast water is flowing.

A river gage records data every 15 to 60 minutes. The information is sent to the United States Geological Survey (USGS) by telephone, radio, or satellite. The data is collected at about 4,500 locations around the United States.

The information gathered by river gages is used by the National Weather Service. The data lets forecasters know which rivers are at, or near, flood stage. City emergency managers also use the information to warn people to get out of an area before a flood becomes dangerous.

People who operate dams use river gage data too. They can open a dam if more water flows away from an area. This can help reduce a flood's impact.

a gaging station along the Suwannee River in Florida

FACT

The USGS began collecting information about water levels in 1895.

How a River Gage Works

SATELLITE OR RADIO TRANSMITTER

GAGE HOUSE: Information about water height is collected inside a gage house. The gage house is built along a riverbank.

STAGE READING AND RECORDING EQUIPMENT: Recording equipment keeps track of the water level.

RIVER AND WELL LEVELS ARE THE SAME.

INLET PIPES: Water comes into the well through inlet pipes.

WELL: At the bottom of a gage house is a well. The water level in the well is the same as in the river.

ANTENNA: A satellite antenna sends data about water height to the USGS.

SHELTER: A shelter protects the equipment that measures water height.

CURRENT METER

A current meter at a gage station also gathers information about a river. It measures how much water is flowing past the station. This is called discharge.

Chapter 4

MAJOR FLOODS

The Deadliest U.S. Flood

Lake Conemaugh was created when the South Fork Dam was built. It was about 2 miles (3 km) long and 1 mile (1.6 km) wide. Johnstown, Pennsylvania, was 14 miles (22.5 km) away, in the valley below the dam.

On May 31, 1889, heavy rains swelled the river that carried water into Lake Conemaugh. The lake level rose. When the dam broke, 20 million tons (18.1 million metric tons) of water cascaded into the valley.

OTHER SIGNIFICANT FLASH FLOODS

OREGON
JUNE 14, 1903—More than 240 people are killed, and the town of Hepner is crushed by a wave 40 feet (12 m) high.

CALIFORNIA
MARCH 12, 1928—The 200-foot (61-m) concrete St. Francis Dam built by the city of Los Angeles in the mid-1920s collapses. Water rushes for more than 50 miles (80 km) down the San Francisquito Canyon, tearing out bridges and killing more than 450 people.

SOUTH DAKOTA
JUNE 9, 1972—Fifteen inches (38 cm) of rain falls in five hours in the Black Hills. A flash flood in Rapid City kills 238 people and costs more than $164 million in damage.

COLORADO
JULY 31, 1976—One hundred forty four people drown and $30 million in damage is done when a stationary thunderstorm causes Big Thompson Canyon to flood.

WYOMING
AUGUST 1, 1985—Six inches (15 cm) of rain falls in three hours. The resulting flood leaves 12 dead and does $61 million in damage in Cheyenne.

OHIO
JUNE 14, 1990—A 30-foot (9-m) wall of water is created after 4 inches (10 cm) of rain falls in less than two hours in Shadyside. The flood kills 26 people and costs $6 to $8 million in damage.

The flash flood picked up everything in its path. Houses, animals, and people were swept up as it rolled through four towns. By the time the flood reached Johnstown, it was a wall of water and debris moving at 40 miles (64 km) per hour.

Some of the debris got stuck on a bridge. It created a pile that was 40 feet (12 m) tall and covered 30 acres (12 hectares). Eighty people trapped in the debris were killed when it caught fire.

This image from Johnstown flood house pierced b

Some people swept up by the wave never found. The flood and the fire at t killed 2,209 people and destroyed 1,600 It was the deadliest flood in U.S. history

Deadly Floods around the World

NETHERLANDS: A storm on the North Sea sent a surge of water over dikes and into the Netherlands on February 1, 1953. The floods killed 1,800 people.

POLAND: The Oder River lies on the border between Germany and Poland. Canals and wooden and stone walls were built to try to contain it. In 1997 rain strained the walls and canals. The river overflowed in a number of areas. Thousands of people had to leave their homes, and more than 90 people drowned. More than 1,200 cities, towns, and villages were affected by the flood. In 2010 the river flooded again, killing more than 20 people.

CHINA: Each year strong storms hit southern China in late spring and summer. These storms often cause flooding of the Yangtze River. The river winds across more than 3,900 miles (6,276 km) and carries more water than any other river in China.

In 1998, more than 4,100 people were killed and 18 million had to leave their homes. The disaster caused $38 billion in damage. The Three Gorges Dam was finished in 2009. It was hoped that the dam would control the flooding along the river. Heavy rain, however, caused flooding again in 2010. More than 1,000 people were killed.

BANGLADESH: Bangladesh had a terrible flood in 1998. Two-thirds of the country was covered with water. Seven hundred people died. Many people died from disease that spread because of a lack of clean water. The floods destroyed crops and left 21 million people without homes.

INDIA: Large amounts of rain fall in India during the summer monsoon season. In July 2005, more than 37 inches (94 cm) of rain fell on Mumbai in one day. More than 1,000 people were killed.

The Costliest U.S. Flood

The 1993 Mississippi River flood was one of the worst disasters the United States has ever seen. The flood impacted nine states and spread over 400,000 square miles (1,035,995 sq km). Damage to property and other losses totaled $20 billion. It was the costliest flood in U.S. history.

Flooding began in early June and lasted throughout the summer. The ground was already wet and rivers were full by June 1. Then more rain started to fall, and it kept falling. The upper Mississippi area had rain every day between late June and late July.

The rain made rivers rise. Tens of thousands of people had to leave their homes. Fifty people died. The flood destroyed 50,000 homes and covered more than 15 million acres (6 million hectares) of farmland. Bridges and roads were washed away. Airports closed. For an entire summer, the flooding upset life in the Midwest.

Mississippi River on August 14, 1991, at normal levels

—Illinois River

—Mississippi River

Missouri River —

Mississippi River on August 19, 1993, at flood levels

TIMELINE FOR THE GREAT FLOOD OF 1993

MID-JUNE: Eight inches (20 cm) of rain fall across the Upper Midwest. Rivers flood in Minnesota and Wisconsin.

EARLY JULY: Iowa gets hit with record rain. Many storms bring up to 8 inches (20 cm) of rain.

JULY 9: Des Moines, Iowa, is hit hard by floods.

JULY 12: The Mississippi River crests at 43 feet (13 m) at St. Louis, tying a record.

MID-TO LATE JULY: Heavy rains fall in North Dakota, Nebraska, Kansas, and Missouri. Rivers in these states and South Dakota have record floods.

JULY 20: The Mississippi River reaches 47 feet (14 m) at St. Louis, a new record.

JULY 27: The Missouri River crests at 48.9 feet (14.9 m), setting a new record.

AUG. 1: The Mississippi crests at 49.47 feet (15 m) in St. Louis, another new record.

FACT

Iowa usually gets 30 to 36 inches (76 to 91 cm) of rain between April and August. In 1993 some areas got almost 48 inches (122 cm) of rain.

Some homes were almost completely underwater during the 1993 Mississippi River flood.

The Most Destructive U.S. Flood

The Mississippi River became a raging force of death and destruction in spring 1927. Two hundred people died and 600,000 lost their homes. The ruin stretched from Cairo, Illinois, to New Orleans, Louisiana.

1. Problems began in the summer and fall of 1926 when heavy rain fell. Rivers that flow into the Mississippi began to rise. On January 1, 1927, the Mississippi reached flood stage at Cairo, Illinois.

3. Because of this flood, the Flood Control Act of 1928 was passed. The United States government began looking at ways to control floods along the Mississippi and other rivers. Levees were built to protect areas from high water. Floodways sent excess water away from the Mississippi. Dams were built to hold water back. This work attempted to prevent another disaster.

The Mississippi River is more than 2,000 miles (3,200 km) long.

One tragedy of the Great Mississippi Flood of 1927 was the way African-Americans were treated. Some were forced to build levees. When a levee broke at Mounds Landing, Mississippi, many were killed.

After the levee broke, people crowded onto a levee in Greenville, Mississippi, to escape the water. Blacks were not allowed to leave. They lived in tents and had little food or clean water. When the flood waters receded, African-Americans were forced to help clean up the mud. Many African-Americans left the area after the flood.

2. As the swollen Mississippi flowed south in March and April, more rain fell on the region. There was fear that the rushing water would cause levees along the river to break. The height of the levees was raised in an attempt to keep the water back.

On April 16, a major levee break occurred 30 miles (48 km) south of Cairo, Illinois. The flood covered 175,000 acres (70,820 hectares) with water. Five days later, a levee broke at Mounds Landing, Mississippi. Water flowed through a gash that was 0.75 mile (1.2 km) wide. The next day, downtown Greenville, Mississippi, was covered with 10 feet (3 m) of water. People in the area had to climb onto roofs and into the tops of trees to escape the high water.

The water continued to flow south. In New Orleans, a levee was broken on purpose to keep the water away from the city.

In June and July, the floodwaters began to recede. A record amount of water had flowed downstream from Cairo, Illinois. Flooding stretched from Missouri to Louisiana. The flood caused $230 million in damage.

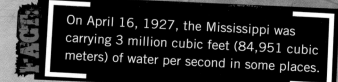

On April 16, 1927, the Mississippi was carrying 3 million cubic feet (84,951 cubic meters) of water per second in some places.

Chapter 5

STAYING SAFE

Flood Safety

DO:

- Listen to National Oceanic and Atmospheric Administration Weather Radio.
- Listen to weather reports on the radio or TV if a flood threatens. Reporters will tell you which areas are in danger of flooding.
- Get to higher ground if you are in an area that may flood. Flood-prone areas include canyons and floodplains.
- Stay away from areas that have flooded.
- Turn around and go the other way if your family is driving and sees a "Road Closed" or "Flooding Ahead" sign.

DON'T:

- Camp or park along a stream.
- Walk, swim, or play in floodwater.
- Wade into a flowing stream past your ankles. You can be knocked down by flowing water that is 6 inches (15 cm) deep.
- Try to drive through a road covered with water. The water may be deeper than it looks, or the road may be washed away under the floodwaters.

FLASH FLOOD WARNING SIGNS

If you are walking or camping along a stream or river, be alert for changes in the water. Leave the area if:
- The water level rises rapidly, and the water becomes muddy.
- You hear a roaring sound upstream.

PLAN AHEAD

Talk with your family about the flood danger in your neighborhood and what you would do in case of a flood. Decide where you would go if you had to get to higher ground.

If a flood watch is issued, gather these items in a flood readiness kit:

- A battery-powered radio
- Flashlights with extra batteries
- Bottled water
- Food that will not spoil
- First-aid supplies

Fighting Floods

Efforts to control floods continue. Cities dig ponds to hold rainwater. Special pavement lets water soak into the soil. Levees are strengthened. The National Weather Service works to improve its forecasts to give people more warning when a flood threatens.

Learning about floods helps people become aware of their danger. Wise decisions must be made to keep people safe from this common but deadly hazard.

Television reporters help keep people informed in the event of a flood.

AFTER A FLOOD

Here are some things people can do to clean up after a flood:

- Clean out mud.
- Drain water from ceilings, walls, and basements.
- Clean with bleach to get rid of germs and the smell of the floodwaters.
- Rebuild damaged walls.
- Throw out soaked carpeting, padded furniture, wallpaper, and books.

FLOOD CONTROL

Here are some ways to control floods:

POROUS PAVEMENT—Water can seep through the pavement and drain into the soil.

RAIN GARDEN—Water pools in the garden and slowly seeps into the ground. Wild flowers and other plants soak up the water through their roots.

SWALE—A grassy, shallow dip in the land collects water during a rainstorm. The water moves slowly through the swale so it can soak into the soil.

DRY POND—A pond that fills with water during a storm.

FLOODPLAIN MAP—A map that shows areas that will likely become flooded if a river rises. Homes should not be built in a floodplain.

SANDBAGS—Bags filled with sand that are piled in front of businesses and homes when a flood threatens. They keep water away for a short time.

RESERVOIR—A lake created when a river is blocked by a dam. The lake's water level can be controlled by opening or closing the dam.

Soldiers are sometimes called in to help clean up after a flood.

GLOSSARY

condense (kuhn-DENSS)—to turn from a gas to a liquid

debris (duh-BREE)—the remains of something that has been destroyed

erosion (ih-ROH-shun)—the process of wearing away rock or soil by water, wind, or ice

glacier (GLAY-shur)—a large, slow moving mass of ice

hurricane (HUR-uh-kane)—a spinning storm with winds of 74 miles (119 km) per hour or more

lahar (LAH-hahr)—a flow of water mixed with debris from a volcano

levee (LEV-ee)—a bank built up to prevent flooding

monsoon (mahn-SOON)—a wind that blows at certain times of the year; during monsoon season, there is very heavy rainfall

radar (RAY-dar)—a system that uses radio waves to detect and locate objects

satellite (SAT-uh-lite)—a spacecraft that circles Earth and takes pictures of the planet from space

storm surge (STORM SURJ)—a dome of water pushed ashore by a hurricane

tsunami (su-NAH-mee)—a giant sea wave

READ MORE

Dwyer, Helen. *Floods.* Eyewitness Disaster. New York: Marshall Cavendish Benchmark, 2010.

Eagen, Rachel. *Flood and Monsoon Alert!* Disaster Alert! New York: Crabtree Publishing Company, 2011.

Oxlade, Chris. *Floods in Action.* Natural Disasters in Action. New York: Rosen Publishing Group, 2009.

Winget, Mary. *Floods.* Forces of Nature. Minneapolis: Lerner Publications, 2009.

INTERNET SITES

FactHound offers a safe, fun way to find Internet sites related to this book. All of the sites on FactHound have been researched by our staff.

Here's all you do:

Visit *www.facthound.com*

Type in this code: 9781429660211

INDEX

48